Robert Sidney Wayland

**The Legend of Maiden Rock**

Robert Sidney Wayland

**The Legend of Maiden Rock**

ISBN/EAN: 9783337391423

Printed in Europe, USA, Canada, Australia, Japan

Cover: Foto ©Andreas Hilbeck / pixelio.de

More available books at **www.hansebooks.com**

OF

# MAIDEN ROCK.

BY

ROBERT SIDNEY WAYLAND.

PHILADELPHIA:

J. B. LIPPINCOTT & CO.

1870.

# CONTENTS.

1* ( 5 )

# THE LEGEND OF MAIDEN ROCK.

## I.

### OONTUM.

FOR many lands within its rocky bourn
　　Along the north and sedgy barriers down,
Unnumbered years the mighty river rolled
Its drowsy volume through the ancient world.
Here in the quietness of earlier times
The dusky children of an untold race
Over the ripples plied the shivering bark
Making the waves to run.　But loud and long
Came other sounds from raging beasts of prey,
That from the hills had come with stealthy tread
Slow creeping down to lap their noonday drink.
For when each one had quenched its thirsty maw,
With throat bent back it sent the thunders crashing
Up the glens, caught in the sounding banks,
Till rolling, they died way down the hollow land.
But often through those listless solitudes,
And o'er the damps lying along the edge,
A wilder note, the yell of lawless war,
Echoed from dark recesses and still nooks.
Then was the reign of ancient silence broke ;

( 7 )

Or when some lonely hawk or fisher-bird
Dipt in the waves, then shaking off the spray
With its bright burden flapped up to the cliffs;
Or a seeming nobler flight, the eagle, flew
Shrill screaming over the margin in its wake.

Here by this sea that swings atow'rd the main
A people lived in times long since gone by;
A people, like the land, rugged and wild
Before it came to us.   And here they had lived
So long that even their coming was a doubt,
And knew they not who their progenitors were,
Except in mythic lay they told of one
Who came down from that shining seat above
When all the world was young, and placed them there:
And hence the name of children of the Spirit
(That mighty Power unseen) was the only name
They knew themselves by, and 'twas all they knew;
While vague tradition dim and oft obscured,
Like some old, half-forgotten nursery tale,
Came to their help and was their oracle.

They came, they lived their life, they passed away—
This is their history, this their epitaph.
No glowing records marked their untold deeds,
Nor pond'rous monuments fashioned in great art
Reveal their wars and victories to these times.
Perhaps at once they held affinity
With those old nations that have gone to death,
And then within the darkness that fell down,
Wrapping the world up for a thousand years,
They lost all knowledge like and so sunk lower;

This is conjecture merely, and we know
They lived and had their day and then went off.

Here lies a lesson for ourselves to learn ;
For what is man compared to all of these ?
Here nations rose in number as the stars :
They drew the little breath allowed to life,
Then each was laid beneath the yearly leaves
To moulder back to little nothingness.
How vain, how vain our greatness and our hopes;
Just let us look calm one moment at death
Then drop our head down at our feebleness.
Nor can we more.   Save for a little while
For us none will weep, none miss us or care ;
These too will go, and others still, and we,
Untold, forgotten, lost to life, will rot;
And o'er this fleshy temple of the mind
The dank and hateful weeds will bear their seed
And hide the earth from day: but it is just,
For of the tears a dying nation gets
From others when it passes from the sight
A single shaking man should not claim one.

Yet nations have their hearts sometimes like men,
And some mark'd action will reveal their grief
And touch a cord of pity in each one.
Here is an act that comes not down by rote,
Nor fashioned into taste by learned hands
Fastidiously.   It, unadorned and plain,
Was kept from ancient times by simple means:
A homely story, told by common ones
Around the fires at night.   It helped for years

To quiet mightier passions in the breast
Of wandering ones bereft.   The tales of war
Were all forgotten to them and had died
As dies a whisper in a mighty hall,
And touched the sense no more, but still they kept
And told this little story of the heart
Which brought more feeling to a scattered tribe
Than all the triumphs of their warriors brought.

In this broad valley there were many tribes,
And that good Spirit that ever loves his own,
That keeps the harmless dove safe from the hawk,
And saves the seedling in its folded coat,
Had given them food and raiment all their own.
But they were not content, and still they longed
(With longing suited with their low desires),
Till time had made a glory, false indeed
To that true passion of the higher soul;
But they did not discern, and glory here
Was for the strong and such as ruled by force.
They got their lessons from their own wild world:
That latent spark which lies in every breast
Struck into fire to see the brutes contend,
And when the weakest one went to the ground
They saved the other as a thing of sense.
Nor can we look in hatred on their love:
This feeling is inherent in all men,
And comes as surely as we are born depraved;
For long before the tower on Shinar's plain
Rose up in stately grandeur toward the sky,
Glory—an evil seed of that fell pride
Through which a wicked angel was cast out

Into the lake of fire, who by his fall
Brought suffering, pain, and death on all of us—
Was nurtured into life and grew our bane.

In time of peace a tribe dwelt by the stream
In conelike lodges, made of bark and moss,
Lying like beehives in a pleasant vale,
With walls of green hills on the northern side,
While on the other bluffs rose like a sea
When winds are steady; to the left, the stream.
Behind them, eastward, was a line of wood
That closed, as twilight closes into night,
Into a forest, wild, and wilderness.

Far to the others round this tribe was known
As one whose boast was of its deeds in strife,
And all its warriors followers of a chief
Whose love was war and whose command was law.
For Oontum's mother taught him on her knees,
By little tales that grow like dreams in shape,
The way in which true glory could be found.
Told how his fathers, chieftains of renown,
Were in those regions past the bounds of life,
Now resting from their deeds on downy furs,
While braves stood round with hand and ear intent
To do their bidding quick with cheerfulness,
And how the cowards upon the darkened shores
Walked, fearing ever, and were not content.

And Oontum press'd the lesson to his heart,
And followed it as some their schoolday's hope
Follow until it grows a part of life.

And long before his limbs were solid grown
His wigwam held the trophies of his strength
In shape of clotted remnants of cleft skulls
Hanging from long, coarse, tangled raven hair,
Strung round the walls by way of ornament.

Thus Oontum ruled the tribe by his own will.
His words in peace were law; his warlike scream
Was answered by a thousand like his own.
Then seemingly quick behind each rock and tree
Within the forest gloom there soon peeped forth
The brilliant foretops of the dusky clan.
Then showed each naked body all besmeared
With herbs and dyes and daubs of colored clay
Put on with spareless hands in curious shapes
To make them feared and dreaded; for the chief
Delighted in the din and fury of war,
And frowned down fierce on those who loved it not
And said by act and word they were not brave.
And when the autumn spread its food abroad,
And river, valley, plains, and rolling hills
Were all alive with sounds of wilder life,
He made them hunt and gather home the game
To feed the better ones throughout the gloom.
These did their duty well; and when the frost
Had robbed the sumac of its velvet plumes
The corn was gathered and the meat was dried,
The robes were piled in corners, and their homes
Fitted for comfort and the lolling ease
Of idle heroes resting on their deeds.

And Oontum's children were with him apart
Save one his only daughter.   She was one

With all the tender nature of her kind.
She was a blossom from the mighty trunk
As Jephtha's was to Israel's eye
In days of old.   And Nona Oontum loved
With all his soul, and loved her as his own;
For strength and manhood always do look down
On innocence with kindness, how much more
When added is a father's love and felt his trust
For her he deems the sweetest of them all.
And Nona's brothers deck'd out for the wars,
With huge rings pendent from their nose and ears,
Would five times stoop their stalwart bodies down
To put a kiss upon their sister's lips
Before they raised their clubs up in their wrath.

And Nona was their happiness and pride,
The old men's joy, the idol of them all,
She made them happy in her ringing laugh,
And cast a charm around like a light.
She seemed in her own sweet beauty from above;
Like one that haunts us from an unseen land
And then but in our dreams.   So modest too
And tender was she, like some fragile flower
That needs support and care, and thus she sought
For things by nature here on which to lean
To share her love with, as the vine is taught
To cling by tendrils to some other stem
That holds it kindly from the wrathful wind.
What thing was friendless, lowly, wandering, meek,
Claiming a tear or asking for a smile,
To her was dear and of her family one.
The youngling doves that built about their lodge

Knew her voice distant, and the timid fawn
To her caresses bent its slim arch'd neck
Without a fear, and with its eyes spoke to her;
While from her tread the tiny flower not broke,
She stept so soft to save it, as she tript
Would raise its head up in the wilderness.
In evening when she past the lodges gray
The old men praised her for their own lost ones,
And called and blest her in their doting hearts
For a good spirit—and such she was to them.
She ministered to those of her own kind
Whom none cared for ; all were alike to her.
In pain no sufferer raised his head uncared
By her when times were tranquil, and she helped
When war was over bind the warriors' wounds.
To these she was as in our day so oft
Was some good Sister by the low hard bed
Of a hurt soldier that rested from his wound
Dreaming a shapeless dream ; so when his hurt
Shook him by spells, he, raising up his head,
And seeing the features of that minister
In prayer over him, thought of peace,
And looked on her as on an angel of Heaven.
She mourned with those who had a cause to mourn,
And joyed with them who in their hearts rejoiced.

And Nona's beauty in her outward form
Matched well the beauty of her mind and heart,
And beauty always is more beautiful
To other ones when these do go together.
Her body was not large, but perfect made,
Straight and erect, and not deformed by care.

Her chest was wide, full-busted, and her neck
Uncreased and round and sloping gently down
As slopes a little hillock into the earth.
Her face within it bore an angel grace
Unhurt by evil thoughts; around her mouth
There was a smile that played half seriously,
That would have turned to laugh or pity quick.
False pride so common was not hers, but pride
That makes one better and dearer; and one could see
Upon her tawny cheek the current and flow
Of young and lifeful blood.  Nor was there need
Of pressure and of pain to slim a waist
Made slim by nature ; and her garments too
Were fashioned not in vanity, though they showed
A sweeter beauty not intending it :
A peeping breast struggling over a band
From which her frame grew wider, and half hid
The rounded shoulder and arm.  But sweeter still
Was motion that went with her as that grace
The old love poets sang of; which they said
That once in ancient regions of the world
Followed the maidens whom they wished to laud.

And Oontum gloried in his daughter's form,
And long before she was intended for it
He had her marriage-day arranged for her.
Then to a warrior, Saunup, an ally
In forays and in war, she was to go ;
And Oontum thought it was a noble gift,
And by the union it would bring about
'Twould strengthen his own house by other props
And keep her place secure.  But she knew not

While in her tender years of this resolve
Made for her peace and coming happiness;
So loved him not.   But Saunup loved the maid
Much as a sister one this day would love,
But not as one whose mind was like his own.
Yet had it come that Nona was his mate,
He would have treated her in such a way
As men at those times held their wives to heart.
And many a native maid, princess or peer,
Would have been happy then for Saunup's smile.
The glory of his arms; his manly frame,
Covered with sinewy network, and his place,
These would have brought devotion and firm trust.
From such as he those tender-hearted ones
Seldom or never turn, but learn to love;
And any one who had trusted in his strength
Might nestle on his arms her lonely head
And there, secure, rested from every harm.

But in a given channel runs not love.
Love is a restless torrent that breaks out
Beyond the bounds of ordinary ways
Impetuously, and will not be assuaged.
One might as well with handfuls of quick earth
Go stop the stream bursted beyond its banks
As smother love with paltry reasonings.
How many ones there are who think they love,
How few there be who know even the word!

But so it was with Nona that she loved
Another one than him her father wished,
A hunter of the tribe that she was of,

And one of those the chieftain held beneath
In place among them, and through mere mischance
It happened at the first to come about.
For once when Nona gayly went to the wood
That skirted the village, with some other girls,
They gathered flowers, and chased the humming-birds
That flew from wild-cups out till they were tired
And some were scattered farther in the deep.
Then Nona sitting down beneath a tree
One by one pluck'd the leaves, which as they fell
Dotted the garnishing stars, and in her hand
The folded bulbs on which she ever mused,
Thinking on what they held and how they seemed
To chatter a language in their sweet perfume,
Carelessly waited on their coming up.
And as she rested there she did not hear
A lonesome step come up to where she lay
Until it was 'most upon her, and as she looked
She saw some one above her gazing down
In wonderment at her.  She was so scared
That for a moment-like her heart stood still;
She could not talk, frightened, although she saw
That he was startled too and in a fright
And stood a looking much like one condemned;
But in his hand he held a bunch of flowers,
And this attracted her, for it seemed strange
That he had flowers—a man have flowers! strange.
By seeing them her heart was quieted
On sudden, for they had the same effect
Upon her heart as has the juice distilled
Of purple foxgloves on the weakly hearts
Of those who have a sickness.  Still he stood

Wrapped in an awe for that long moment there,
Not knowing what to say or what to do;
And she knew not; till, trembling in his tongue,
He, like a child that tells the simple truth,
Which, thinking not on the word but on the gift,
Does prattle what is nearest, said at last,
"Our princess take these buds: I did not see you—
I knew not where I went." He said no more,
But as he past he dropt them by her side
And into the forest vanished at a turn.

Her eyes were down: she knew not that he had gone,
All was so sudden, her surprise so great;
And when she looked to see him standing there
No person was before her, none was near.
But on her mind there was a form impressed,
Like to the image painted on dead eyes,
That time could not efface: a boyish frame,
With a high forehead and a tender eye,
His head bent sideways in astonishment,
His hands upraised, and then a bunch of flowers.

Till then had Nona loved 'most everything
For its own sake, but now there came full fast
Another feeling, but she knew not what,
That stole upon her almost unaware.
She reached out for the offering that he had made,
Took it and kissed it as a thing of life,
And put it to her breast and cherished it
Love-like, making her thoughts upon it. And when
The wandering maids were going home again
The others wondered why she was so sad

And seeming thoughtful while their laughter rose.
But answers to their questions she had not,
Or else they were evasive and were turned
Upon a subject foreign to their talk.
For in her reticence she mused and mused,
And felt unkindly as she was disturbed;
For by comparison his going off
Had left her stand as one who walks alone
In night-time when across a cloudless sky
A meteor makes a shining path of fire
And breaks upon the zenith; then when he
Who saw the heavens lit up suddenly bright
Looks and beholds the scattered flakes descend
When darkness comes again, and, lo! he thinks,
While still the vision is before his sight,
The earth is darker than it was before.

While modesty is woman's loveliest trait,
A man shows nature in his bashfulness
Which often draws disdain; but some are so
Ev'n from their infancy—a better trait
Than boldness is, though seldom thus we reason.
Boldness is veiled as was that fallen crew
Sang by old Milton, while the seraphs stoop
Bashful and sinless in the presence of God.
And nature is the same throughout the world:
Nor can we marvel greatly that there lived
At where the mind was cramped many of souls
Who in thoughts wandered farther from their sphere
Than those we read of, and who laid them down
And died, conscious the world was all too small
For their conception.   Such the lengthened train

From him who told of far-resounding Troy,
The echoing echo of whose wars but still
Sounds round the world ringing; the clanging fields
By rolling Simois, and the dreadful wrath
That left in mighty heaps the unburied bones
Of perished heroes lying along the shores
Of distant Xanthus; by him of the song
Arms and the man, he who by heartless fate
Impelled, and Juno's rage, drove to the shores
Of Italy, from whence the glory of Rome ;
By him to whom his people, aliens! gave
Taunts (that to age and exile) and disgrace
For shame they heaped upon him; and for this
He left her name in kindly recompense
Side by side with that fair city of bliss
Whose jewel'd towers and sapphire battlements
Holds in the splendor of Heaven; even by him
That wayward singer who cheers our weary way,
To other ones beyond the sounding main
In dreary countries where the light of sense
Shone never on the soul;—all those whose minds
Are known to fame and those more numerous
Who have died unheard, but even who themselves
In secret grieved over their loneliness.

Such was this hunter    Timid like a girl
He hung his head and felt like any of them
To think upon himself.   Nor was it strange
That old men slowly shook their weakling heads,
And talked foreboding of his future years;
That in their many changing prophecies
They told with wondrous wisdom how that ill

Hung over him and surely was his doom.
For separate from the others was his mind
Which was not suited with his way of life,
But grew as some fruit fit for man to have
Grows on an arid waste and there decays,
Its worth unknown and gone. All was a doubt.
A man in darkness could approach his thoughts
Who, lost in some far labyrinth under ground,
Gropes for the light of day, while all around
The smooth and pond'rous walls he feels his way
And rounded pillars which he cannot clasp
For mightiness: then walls and walls again
All incoherent spread their magnitude,
Till in despair he feels his littleness,
Yet knows the blessed light shines far away,
But all is dark to him. Thus, as his brain
Expanded with the going of the years,
The doubt was more his own, and all he knew
Was what the greatest man of heathen times
Said is our wisdom, Nothing can be known.

He did not like the people as they lived,
Nor with them think to find the peace he sought;
But these he oft forsook to find a spot
Where nature was harmonious with his soul;
He would have lived with his own dark thoughts rather
Deep in the wood·than be with them with theirs.
This was his nature, and even when a boy,
Devoid of any care, he did not mix
Among his playmates as they trained their limbs
In sports of puny war over the green;
But these he left to have their joys alone

While he had his.   These were in solitude,
Where quiet stilled him with the outer world,
Or lulled him down in listless reveries
With rippling murmurs, solitude of life.
Or on a bank of moss under a tree
Aged and hoary, dim with lichen gray,
The misty dress of time (the garlands sad
Of ancient days), and venerable for age
Beyond frail man, while ever round about
The whispering leaves and lonely drone of bees
The live-long summer day made the mind dream.
There often would he rest; there in his heart
Was laid the germ of such an alien fruit
As nurtured has been death to many ones.
There to his vision rose those forms laid low,
And there through vistas long a land appeared,
Serene and fair, in which their spirits rested,
In happiness unknown; for what is loved
By heathen souls within the flesh is loved
In image—perfect in their paradise.

Moren that morning was a-hunting game
With other hunters but till they past on by
And left him lagging in the wood behind,
Among the whitened blossoms.   When he had filled
With scarlet buds his hands, and stars of day,
And little stems which other ones called weeds,
He made them to a bundle prettier far
In careless taste than had they been arranged.
Then with his eyes bent down for many a step
O'er the rough land he trod without a thought
Until he suddenly woke, but woke as one

That wakes to dream again ; then he stood
Frightened and lost before the princess' eyes.

Then what he said was spoken with the thought,
Like lightning come and gone ere we are aware.
Then as a man that scares at echoes made
By his own footfalls in an empty place
Where all is night and stillness, was he scared,
Nor did he stop till he was hid secure
In his own lodge behind the common street.
There raged the tempest in his mind again
Lest she was angry at him, but the thought
Ev'n made the sweetness of that short-lived look
Like sunny gleams come up before his sight.
Yet trust himself he could not to a thought,
Well knowing the changing nature of the world,
For often had he found himself at ease,
And then the knowledge that it would not last,
Creeping, thief-like, stole all his ease away,
And made him feel more sad and miserable.

But he had never known the earth to hold
So fair a creature as he saw in her,
And though she was the talk of all the tribe,
He knew her merely by the outward sign
That tells of inward greatness, and he felt
That he could follow her for evermore,
To do her bidding as they did the men's—
Yet else than give his service or his life
He felt himself unfitted, and he dared
Not even hold a thought he loved, for when
The image of that one came upward to him

He crushed the thought as though it were a sin—
A stain that spots the conscience; then he went
More often to the wood, and stay'd there longer,
Trying to learn from out the wide-spread book
Knowledge so deep that none can comprehend;
To seek in darkness what was not revealed,
A clew to ravel that deep mystery,
The deepest of all mysteries and the saddest.
He grew still shyer, and he kept himself
From contact with the others; for his part,
He would have lived and died in his despair
Before he would have told what was his hurt.

Not so with Nona, for the more she thought,
And as the space grew longer from that time
When all her thoughts were jarred and ill-confused,
Till after grew they into one known form,
Had she within her felt that longing more
To see him once again and feast her eyes.
And though the flowerets were all faded now,
She kept them still, and loved them as her own,
As we do love a picture dim and gray
That calls to mind the face of one who stays
In some far country other than our own.
And in the flowers she saw the heart of him
Who spoke and gave, and all her days were long.
She went about the lodges oftener now,
And question here was made by her for him,
But asked in such a way that they who heard
Thought that she scarcely spoke in earnestness.
Thus many days dragg'd onward till it chanced
A time was coming, and she had a hope,

And came it after waiting, for the chief,
Calling a council of the braves in which
All were to appear upon the open ground,
For fear of his displeasure, Moren came
From out the place of his obscurity
Caring for none nor wishing any care.

Then in that morning early Nona rose,
And in an anxious fever outlived the dawn
That slowly stole across the eastern world.
Then with the morning people came and came
While she looked vainly for the expected one
By many maidens near the chieftain's throne.
But as we near the grave sweeter is life ;
The haven dearer from a troubled sail ;
The later some long hope is realized
The joy is greater when it comes at last.
So Nona was more happy in the sight
Of him whose coming was so long delayed
After her silent waiting ; for she had looked
To every corner for him till her hope,
In conjuring up some fearful accident,
Was flagging almost down into despair ;
But all this passed away when he appeared
With hasty step to join the scattered crowds
Collecting close to hear the chieftain's will.

When Nona saw she felt herself relieved
And lightened of a burden that bore down,
And felt a tinge throughout her every nerve
As though she could have shouted.   When he stood
With folded arms back from the thicker crowd

With fortitude in weakness she went to him,
Thoughtless what to say, or why she went;
But with her tongue aflight with hasty words,
"If I mistake not once you gave me flowers.
Are you not he?"   To hear so sweet a voice
Was Moren moved, and looked to see who spoke:
But eyes spoke more in one short lapse of time
Than tongues could have described within a life.
"I did; you will pardon me," he said confused.
"No pardon, for I love them—love all flowers,
And those were very pretty."   And she looked
From under her long eyelashes to her wrist
Whereat she with a trinket idly toyed.
She stood a moment thus while neither spoke.
Then Nona said to him, "I thank you for them;"
And Moren nodded, but he spoke no word,
When she, joining some passing ones who called,
Lost herself to him in the changing throng.

Thereat the first time when he caught her eye
His senses were all dazzled by its glance,
As birds they say are sometimes lost with fear,
For hers were fired with that celestial love
Whereof the more we look the more of Heaven.
And lightning never made a sudden wreck
Of a tall kingly oak out on a waste
Quicker or more complete than that bright flash
Changed his old love and shaped his destiny.
But long the words she spoke remained with him,
As a last kiss upon some dear loved lips
With us does live forever.   So he loved.

Then when they were ranged in circles round the chief
He raised his voice and spoke to them of war.
"A war-cloud gathers on our borders near
And is about to break.  I now propose
To lead you, braves, against an ancient foe.
I wish you all to come that can bear arms
To break his strength.  Saunup's tribe, following him,
Goes with us and will share us in our fame.
An age's glory will be with our arms
When we have strangled even the smallest babe,
Not leaving one to tell of their disgrace.
Let those who talk of hating war for fear
Remain behind and keep gray company,
Protect the squaws, and sometimes get them food,
And make a feast for us when we come back.
Who goes make ready ; by the changing moon
Our cover then must be the leaves and sky."

Then one loud shout went upward from the throng
Like thunder rolling on the distant wind,
That showed their hearty assent to what he said.
Then the wild shout woke Moren, and with a start
He shook that lethargy from him, for till now
His reason was lost to every outward thing.
And with the shout the tension holding them
Snapp'd, when all dispersed like feathery clouds
Slow breaking from a storm where rain is spent,
Where off in little groups they talked the news,
Greeting each other, while their compliments
Incessantly came in ways they had of their own,
For manners came scarcely by effort, but
Naturally are inborn before they are bred.

The village now from night to morn, again
From morn to night in days that intervened
From now till when the warriors should go forth,
Was all alive with bustle; but before
The morning came when they should take the field
Their wizard priests were busy in their arts,
And smoke of sacrifice continually—
A sign propitious of their sure success—
Curled upward towards the seat of all their power.
The days were passed in feasting, and the nights
Spent out in deep debauch and revelries,
With dances, music, and exciting yells.
Half-clad in garb of war around their fires
They kept their dreadful orgies loud and wild,
Up to the night before it, and in that
Their passions and their excesses knew no bounds.
For all was centered in their dance of war,
That revel when the staidest warrior
Grew frantic o'er the tale repeated oft
That charmed the list'ners' ear.   Then he rose up,
Seized on his arms, and in the vacant air
Struck at the-passing ghosts of chieftains slain
In midnight fight in some far-distant fray.
Or still with fiendish pride exultingly sang
Of how they inflicted pain on captive foes,
And how they would on these.   Then little eyes
Looked on in worship to the godly power,
And timid maidens told to lovers' ears
How they felt envious at the old men's fame.

A level plat, fronting the council lodge,
Extended in a square across the town,

And here they held their feasts.   Within its midst,
Like some lone pillar on a foreign coast,
Arose the stake, the symbol of their joys.
'Round this they danced, and when the night arrived
That was the last one ere they started off,
A score of heaped-up fires, flaring and red,
Blazed on the square and shot their crimson beams
Across the plat far into the night;
While in the glimmering darkness from the stake,
Seated upon the ground in circling rows,
The grave musicians sat with bended backs,
And tuned their dissonance with the female screams.

Then fifty braves, the choicest of the tribe,
Dress'd for the field, advanced.   First low they bent,
Their feathery scalp-locks brushing on the ground;
Then to each side in measured, stately tread,
Their long limbs swinging to each supple joint,
They bowed their bodies down: now high their crests
They toss'd in air, and down each naked back
Flapped the long hair with each quick jerk and toss.
They swung their arms aloft at every note
As fancy should suggest, or lowly down
Let them drop in company with their voice.

There was no melody in their grating noise,
Nor in their voice, nor yet devoid of rhythm
Was the wild burden which they forced aloud
In consonance with discord.   Like the laugh
In the wild ravings of a maniac crowd
Heated within their blood, uprose each note
In quick succession from their upturned mouths,

3*

" Hi, ha-hah, hu-ah, ha-hah," to the strokes
Beat on the leathern gongs, and the sharp clack
Of clapping hands struck by the list'ners round,
To whose fast measure kept each heavy foot
As intricately moved the separate bodies
Among the others, as in the summer sun
The insects fly above the stagnant pools.
While quicker beat the music, and with the noise
The braves became impetuous, and they danced
Faster and faster, and louder came each voice
Inciting the rest to every one engaged.
The wood upon the blazing fires piled high
Scattered the flickering sparks along the sky,
And colored the smoke to clouds of running blood
Waving deep into each other, while below
Each darksome body caught the infective glare
And seemed more hideous and more terrible far;
Till Oontum with the hatchet struck the stake,
When the dance ceased and all the noise was stilled.

The chieftain then related of his wars,
Told of the perils he had passed from home
Among the dangerous tribes, and how by art
He'd brought as tributaries nations old
But for the pleasure that he found in war.
Then heated furious when he show'd to them
The fire of burning lodges lick the heavens,
With all their inmates turned out into th' wood ;
And how they bound to rocky cliffs up high
The bodies of their warriors of renown,
And how the vultures picked their bones for food,
And whetted their beaks against the fallen skulls,

Still ending that this war would be his best,
And till his death his glory should grow with his years.


And ever as he said his deeds of might
The other ones applauded.  When he was done,
Once more the company of the braves swung round
Till the black stake was struck which bade them cease,
When Saunup sang his exploits in these words :


" I am a warrior and a chieftain too.
My work is war and my delight is war.
Often have I fought : many scalps I have brought
From braves I killed.  I killed a mighty chief,
He who was king of the Crows.  I scalped him.
I covered my face with his blood.  As for his scalp,
I hung it round my neck.  Then first I danced.
Oh, I am young, but I shall win a fame ;
I will, I will.  My father was a chief,
And he killed many ; but I his son will mind.
I'll go with you to war.  Then when I kill
I'll scalp them, thus.  Och ! I shall make them cry.
I'll lap their blood ; that is sweetest of all.
Then when the war is over I shall rest
A-telling my deeds, while others when they talk
Of bravery, will say, as brave as Saunup."


Loud came the shouting when he told them this,
From all the braves and warriors standing round ;
And soon the place was filled ; louder yet still
Yelled the dark crew around the noisy fires
That crackling blazed and shot their flames up higher.

Then many aspirant told, with boastful threat,
The fame that lay in store which he should win—
This ere the moon would round to its full size.
So all night long they shook the quiet shades
With fierce portents and fiercer sounds of rage,
Which frighted the birds of darkness and awoke
To sounds obscure the caverns of the wood.
And when the gates of heaven in the east were loosed,
And burst the sun in splendor o'er the trees,
They took their march in long and coiling lines
Till the deep forest swallowed them up entire,
While all the females set up bitter moan.

# II.

## SAUNUP.

AND so they went to war to win renown,
And left the village to peace. Then sorrow came,
Staying but like a season, as the skeleton comes
To sit at feasts when all the meats are gone.
Then Moren knew their thoughts, and so he raved
With bitterer hate by far upon his lot,
Because he was no warrior, and because
There was no way of winning fame but this
To satisfy their palates, and the lusts
That grow by thirst of blood.  And it was plain
That he was held unworthy, for the highest
Were those who fought in battle for their name.
Then to the woods he went from sight, there
Wandering about, hated and feared, away
Hid from their haunts among the peaceful ways
Where snakes, and newts, and clumsy ill-shaped toads
Reveled, and brooded the evil birds ;
A hollow place that held a lonely glen
Where Winter dwelt among the somber hills,
Sending his voice upon the restless winds
Throughout the rounding years continually ;
Where nothing grew save such unhappy weeds
As from the hungry land unwholesome spring
Indigenous, poisoning all the air ;
Here ugly gentian blossomed, and in patches,

Friendless and unkind, the nightshade crept
Over the sands which foreign winds had swirled
In little ridges,—wandering here he found,
Half hidden among the mould, a warrior's skull
Colored by time, and thus to it he spoke:

"And this is part of what was one of us.
And is his glory dwindled down to this?
Say, were his battles many, or were few?
Yet matters not, for this is your reward,
Not decent covered with your native earth
O Manito, Spirit, or what name thou hast,
Thou Great Unknown, didst thou thy children make
So free as those dim whispers from thee say?
Or were we made like game to be ensnared?
Was that part in us which is kin to thee
Made to be ruined and like unto beasts?
And shall our bodies be torn and rent apart
By those who happen to be made more strong?
Shall we be poisoned by them?   Shall we turn
The feeling you gave us into such as theirs?
'Tis like your owner had a lively taste
Of his own greatness, and he thought him chief
Of earth and water, yet he could not tell
The reason why the light comes after snow,
Or knew the hidden power that lies hid up
Within a tiny oak-seed.   That is grand.
How funny it is to think that you who lived,
Who couldn't contain your anger, but roared like
          thunder,
And withered poor creatures with your lightning eyes,
Should take the kick I give you.   Chuck! Ho, so!

A handsome eye that lizard makes you now.
Yet too I pity you, seeing you lie
Amongst the weeds—this from my other self,
Well knowing that we all are like the clods
Nor have a life within us of our own.
Your eyes don't see the world : you cannot speak ;
You hear me not.   That mighty, mystic thing
Talking within us ever,—is that dead ?—
As thus we call it, dead ? dead    How strange ! dead.
When as the winter fires consume the wood
Where goes the vapor?  Is the vapor lost?
A world is sure within us, and another,
A happier life dwells in it : in this world
I live, nor arms, nor fame, or anything
Can draw me from that world in which I live."


But like the sun a ray of shining hope
Lifted these clouds of thought and scattered them off,
And warmed his heart and made his blood run high.
Thus for a little while he stood in day.
Soon, very soon, the fire lit by that spark
Kindled, and kindling blazed into a flame,
And wrapped itself around the hearts of both.
Then Moren left his hidden place to walk,
Putting himself and all the world aside
To get a glance from Nona and a smile.
Then every morning would she find some flowers
Tastefully made lying upon the path
On which she walked to catch the scented air
Of sweetly summer, blown from myriad balms
That perishing died over the western fields.
But in among the rest she always found

A sprig of fadeless laurel, then she knew,
In language of the flowers, who they were for.
Thus on from little to more, from thoughts to words,
As none was near to watch her or forbid,
They went the way that lovers easily know,
For though 'twas she who at the first made love,
His grew the stronger as the days grew on,
Till at the last he thought her all his own;
And on his kiss at evening by themselves,
He hanging on her lips, both felt as free
As robins wrangling for a cherry in air.
He saw her soul reflected in his eyes,
And in it read his happiness or doom,
While she believed that all of life was there,
Having no wish by which she would be disturbed.

In these days Moren was much relieved in mind,
As nothing baleful lay across his way,
Till one or two returning from the war
Reported of their actions and made stir
Of how they were successful, how progressed,
And how soon time they would be all returned.
Then he whose mind hung on a balance like,
Moved by the least caprice was made disturbed.
He called the rest unhappy, and himself
Was most unhappy; but never did he cease
To reverence, with all his heartfelt love,
That creature whom he deemed of all most blest,
Yet sometimes had a doubt that all was right;
But with the smallest hope which those make great
He rested feverish for a better day,
With his whole heart put on a fallen word.

Love is the light that bickers from the dark,
Calling to rest the long-benighted man
Wandering; and as he stops before the door,
Fearing to enter lest the master's voice
Bids him again begone, so Moren stood
Encovered by doubt; but in the world he saw
Among the wrecks confused and toss'd about
The love of Nona: saw it as one sees
The little flowerwaif drooping from its thread
Hanging upon the ivy sad and old
That creeps about the donjon which now lies
Razed on the ground with all its mighty towers
Oft'n i' the old land. Nona was otherwise,
For she was ever expectant and her faith
Put in her father's granting her her wish
Was firm and strong if she should importune.
"O what a joy," she thought, "for father's self
When he comes back, and rests him from the war,
To know his Nona has so true a love,
And one so worthy of his house and power."
A woman surely could not brave the world
If hope were taken away; for hope but lives
A lasting remnant of the golden time
When men were fed on fruits the gifts of gods.
Thus hope dwells still in every breast for good.
As in the spring-time, as the days and nights
Hang on a balance, and the raging storms
That cross the tropics sweep the northern world
With angry blasts, making the distant hills
And the low earth dim, while on some peak afar
The sunlight for an instant makes a crown

4

Glorious, is hope the light on lonely hearts
In this dark world of toil and turbulence.

Meantime the war was ended, and once more
The braves rejoiced to see their wigwams rude,
And so they came in splendor all bedecked
In martial glory and a pageant's pride.
First come those ones who had won their fame again,
Their trophies hanging thickly round their waists,
Their bodies soiled with blood, with dinted clubs
Swung on their shoulders, and their bone-tipt spears.
Next, led, the prisoners whom they deigned to spare
For torture, they motionless like and sad,
Being tied with hides and led before the chief,
Who followed with his cold-cut hero face,
Attended by his sons and dignitaries :
He in a mantle fabricked of dried grasses
And brilliant feathers of the forest birds,
With bright bark interwoven, with a fringe
Of fur, got from the otter and the mole,
Around the border of it every way.
Here Saunup was among them with the sons.
Behind of these on litters came the dead
Which they could carry from the ruined field
Back to their homes to give them burial there,
And fill their pyramid of heroic dead.
After these came the others with their arms:
Some bows and quivers had, and some had spears,
Javelins, hooks, and knives of sharpen'd ribs,
And every instrument that could be of use
To torture or to bring pain on the flesh ;
While rose aloft, at many intervals,

The cold, dead human heads, of which the eyes
Seemed still to look down on them. All were dressed
In gear of war, with towering feathers high,
Which the wild eagles shook once in the storms
About their eyries in the mountain cliffs.
They all had rings hanging down from their ears
Upon their shoulders, and from out their noses,
Circling their mouths, through which they grinned
    like beasts,
For all their mouths were black'd around with clay,
And round their eyes were scarlet or like blood.

The people then came out to see them in,
And all along the way their shouts went up,
While drums were beat to make a kind of march,
And rattles of bison-horn and pipes of reed
Threw out their discord as to increase the din.
So when they came within the well-known square,
Now thickly packed around for many deep,
They made their slow way toward the council lodge,
Which rose high on a mound above the rest.
Here were the women placed; this was the spot
Where they should stop, and where for coming days
They should regale themselves, and satiate
To fullness, feasting till their cares were gone.

When Nona saw those ones so dear approach,
The passion in her she could not contain,
But left her stand, and in her gayest dress
Ran forward when the column came in view
And as she crossed the plat in flowing robe
That bent itself to all her rounded limbs,
Her black hair streaming in the wind behind,

Bound from her forehead by a band of gold,
From which a sea-shell rose,—she seemed again
Not of this earth, and every voice was still.
The varied colors of the skies and wood
Waving shone on her, and a girdling belt
Of whiteness bound the folds to fit complete;
And round her arms were bands of virgin gold
Which showed the grains of flinty rocks like pearls.
No voice was heard as 'cross the plat she ran;
And when she reached her father's side he stopped;
Bending his body down in stately pride
To her embrace, about his heavy neck
She threw her arms, and on his angled mouth
Her own, which never yet was falsely pressed,
She pressed with all a daughter's passion felt.
Thereon the crowd, whose pulse is easy moved,
Seized on the moment, for their blood was up,
And every mouth was opened; far and wide
Beyond the happy town the echoes sounded
Among the hollow wood, and all were glad.

When greeting had been ended and they told
To eager list'ners all of that old tale
Of dangers, hardships, and of bitter times,
Now magnified because they were but past—
On that same evening ere they settled down,
Being not so restless as they were all day,
Did Nona's father to him draw her near
To tell her how through all the fruitful war
Had Saunup earned a fame to last for time;
A fame so fit that it deserved her love—
That he should have it; for from a day far back

Before her pretty childhood had gone by
He promised her to him as being most fit
To guard their bud and cherish it in bloom
When it had grown.   " Now after," thus he said,
" I see you sitting by the wigwam door,
And thinking in your mind how he and I
Are far away and fighting side by side,
And ever wishing in your silent heart
For him to come and nestle by your breast,—
To listen while he tells the little ones
Of truant war with all its strange mishaps.
This is the grandest time my heart could wish,
For I am giving all my Nona wants
Which of itself is out of th' other's hope."

Then Nona's eyes were on a sudden enlarged
Under the new excitement, and she said,
Looking to Oontum's face, "O father dear,
Instead of pleasing, you do hurt my heart.
I do not love brave Saunup as you say,
Nor ever had a wish to call him mine ;
But I do love another, whom I know
For my sake even you can learn to love
When you have known him, for he's worthy of it——
(I think sometimes that I am not of him).
He will bring honor to us I know well,
For he loves me with more than common love ;
And I was waiting, hoping, till you came
To tell you of it and to get your will.
And as you love me, father, I do know
That you will grant my greatest wish to me
That ever yet I've had a cause to seek."

4*

'Tis true that Nona was in part confused,
But in the simple nature of her kind,
Confiding all her care and all her hope,
She broke her happy joy to Oontum's ear.

Then Oontum's face did slowly show a frown
To see requited ill his plan matured,
And turned to naught by her he loved the most.
" My Nona," said he with his lips compressed,
" I look upon your love as foolishness—
Whatever it may be as a passing flash
Not worthy of a second thought—nothing at all
Compared with that of him    And so, my bud,
You shall do as I bid you, for I know
The thing that is far better for us all.
As Saunup claims you, on to-morrow's morn
I shall with pleasure place your hand in his,
Yet with a sorrow let it go from mine.
But he will keep you all your living days
As 'comes a chieftain's daughter and a wife."

But Nona's eyes were on the leafy floor,
And but confusedly she seemed to hear—
Heard as some innocent convicted hears.
His silence woke her and she raised her face ;
His that just bore that harsh look was more calm.
Yet could she hardly speak, nor dare she try,
Ill news so sudden breaks the body down.
She raised her arms above her ; down they fell
Upon his shoulders where she hung, and hid
Her head beside his own, and trembled sore.
And there she hung a goodly time ; at last

She slowly found expression, and she cried,
" O father, how you frightened me! I thought
Which time your dear face wore that angry scowl
That all your sullenness was bent on me.
But say it is not so. How could your heart
Be angry at me when I only said
I love not Saunup? Will you kill me quite
By saying I must have him? O take that back,
Dear father, take it back, that bitter word
You did not mean for me. Do only say
You are not angry with me, and kill me not,
O kill me not by saying I am his."

But Oontum loosed her arms with gentleness,
And pushed her from his shoulder where she clung.
Then all uneasy-like, both short and quick,
He said, " Nona, you are his and his alone,"
And left her lying sobbing, head in arms,
Upon a furry seat, while from his mouth
"A passing fancy common to the young"
Came with a settled firmness; but she lay
Through all the lingering hours of that drear night
All lonely, sobbing in her sudden grief,
Wishing that she could die and have her love
Die with her, and that both of them were hid
Out of the sight of all the living world
In that dark valley of the silent dead;
Till by-and-by the morning stars grew dim,
And glowed the embers on their dying fires
Faintly outside whereby the revelers slept.
Then when her body was so tired and racked
Did nature, mother-like, soothe all her pain,

And rocked and lulled her till it was forgot
As in her grief she, weeping, fell to sleep.

The morning came, and with it Oontum came
To see her, thinking she was changed for good,
Or that the suddenness and time he had told
The news to her affected her the most.
His coming broke her sleep and she stood up;
But how that gentle face was marked with grief
Since the last evening when she was so gay!
He was surprised to see her, and exclaimed,
"Why, Nona, how is this?   I came to see
You waiting for me in your best attire
With all the household glad.  What means this change?
Say, are you ill, or wherefore do you grieve?"

Then burst her voice forth in a piercing shriek,
" O father, let me be to die, to die."
And on the floor she lay with body bent.
Nor could be calm or quiet her so much
As find for what she mourned ; but heard her moan
Full sore and passionately at his feet,
Till on the sudden flashed the cause upon him.
Then over her he stooped ; he raised her up,
And on his mighty body let her rest.
Yet soon he petulantly set her down,
With full intent to have his way in this
And then to make her happy as before.

She, left alone, her storm did slow subside.
As one determined inwardly to do,
She rose herself to make her feel more strong.

She called aloud the name of one who came,
Whose duty it was to wait upon her wants,
One trusted by her, and to whom she said,
" Go tell my brother of the eagle eye,
Say to him to come quickly ; tell him too
His sister sent you"—and the girl sped off.
He with the surname Eagle-Eye then came,
A warrior like his father huge and strong,
But with a heart withal that ever beat
Tender for her who was their own.   His mirth
Was stricken down within him when he saw
Her as she was and so unlike herself.
" Why, Nona, what is the matter? say, sweet bud,
What power has crushed you since I saw you last?"
She told him in a manner much composed
The doleful story of her father's will
That went so much against her, ending thus :
" If you, my brother, wish to see me live,
Or if you love me as you say you do,
Or if you even think a good thought of me,
Then tell our father to break off his word
And let me live with mine or not at all."
" Why you," and at the thought he laughed outright,
" Why you, my sister, are a peevish girl      '
To make such fuss at nothing.   Better far
That you were laughing in expectancy
Of better times before you.   And why do you
Fret like a wounded bird at your good luck ?
Where is the one who, placed as you are placed,
Would not be jumping in her heart?   I think
That you, with wiles best known to your own kind,
Do not think half so much as you let on.

Say, is 't not so?"  "Oh, mock me not that way,"
Cried Nona, changed—she not expecting this.
"And do you think that I could be untrue,
And clothe my tongue in such a low deceit?
I thought you knew me better, brother mine."
Then answered he, but not in mirthfulness,
" I did not say it, little one, that you
Had clothed your tongue deceitfully.   Oh, no
So, think you so, I'll wipe that stain away."
Her forehead kissed thereon.   " Now then ; but, if
You love not Saunup (but I trust you do),
What kind of love is yours compared with him ?
Where will you find his like within the world ?
To me the thought has often come, that when
You leave our lodge to give your care to him
You in a little while will be estranged.
Then would I cross my nature and be sad ;
But were you happier, then should I be pleased.
May be he cannot, in a winning voice,
Coo, pigeon-like, his song within your ear
Of never-ending love ; yet he could love
And tell it not in words, but by his acts,
Which come more handy than does gliding speech.
I know his prowess well, and well his strength,
For with my eyes I've seen him lick the blood
From off the scalp-locks of the boldest braves,
As though it were honey dripping from the comb.
Then carried well the name he bore before—
That which he earned when young—the Mountain Cat.
But had you seen him then, his face and arms
Running with others' blood, you would have thought—

Before the night-star showed his evening light—
Thought it your highest glory to be his."

Thus ran he on, as heated by the theme,
But little cared she then to hear the tale ; .
For when she thought of how she'd pledged herself,
Thought also of the troth she plighted once—
Not mockingly, but with her inner heart—
She found a voice to plead her cause, and spoke :

" I have said my wish, and told you of my love,
So talk can never change me ; but if he
And you, my oldest brother, give me off,
Or try to give me off, before that time
Take me to the green, and tie my hands
Behind me, bind my body to a stake ;
Thus burn me up, and gladly will I die,
And think so kindly of you all the while,
For keeping me from lingering out my life."

Her brother knew it was idle to urge on
As she was sure in earnest; for that love
Which makes the strong ones weak, the weak ones
    strong,
Had made her look determined and of will.
And half for pity did he then relent
With promise to do for her what he could.

He sent his brothers to her, and she told
The same to them, and they all pitied her
And said they would prevail as best they could
Upon their father to break off his word

And let her have the only one she wished. .
But, thinking kindly for her all the time,
It was concerted among them that they should,
To comfort her, appear to get it changed,
But really just to ask their father's power
To get the time extended unknown to her,
When, as they thought, a time will make a change
(For on the chief they looked as on their own),
Save one who, though he held his peace about it,
Could not agree to see their sister sold.

They told their father all.   He, like a beast
Brought from the wilds and barred within a cage,
Was ill at ease and could not rid him of it.
And they told Saunup, making it appear
That she was ill, and that the suddenness
Of all had broke her down, but that she would
Within a little time be willing for him.
And this too they told Oontum, who at last
Was willing that the time should be set off,
For he had no suspicion but that she
Would have, not opposing, him whom they wished.

Here Nona's grief began.   The little joy
We think we have is but a doubtful dream—
The more the joy the deeper is the dream ;
Thus when we waken, lo ! the dream is gone,
And life is joyless in our wakeful hours.
Even like the buzzing of a summer fly
That droops at every chill, or dies in pain
Within the grasping of an idle boy,
Is but the changing of our brittle day.

And in the semblance of our catching joy
We hurt our fellow with a deeper grief,
As some men that for pleasure pierce the pin
Clean through the body of an insect bee
To see it writhe, and beat its wings, and tramp
The empty air to free itself, to know
How long it can be dying and yet live,
Are many who to gratify themselves
Do sell the love of others, thinking not
That they be piercing other hearts with barbs
Which pain more than the shiny point of steel
Thrust in its membrane in the flesh would pain ;
Who thinking of advantage, never look
Upon the side reverse until too late ;
And thus intently do they seem the beast
That buffets in its paws its prisoner.
So Nona felt herself a helpless prey,
And felt the hateful barb pierce in her heart,
And felt the chillness gather in her blood,
And felt that other days were but a dream,
And like the fly that struggles to get free
With something in it answering to our hope
She turned herself to Moren.   When one turns
In friendship and for comfort to a friend
In needful times and then no friend is near,
One's grief is full, for even the woodland birds
Do share their frail, high-swinging tenements
With their weak comrades in the pelting storm.

But from the village Moren had gone before
The warriors were returned, and hid himself
Deep in the forest from their hateful gaze.

5

There stay'd until the day of greeting was past
When he beneath the darkness stole to home.
So Nona saw him not.   Then in her heart
She felt, but for an instant, love's remorse,
And wondered, " Is his love a hate that thus
He has gone from me when I miss him most
To tell him of my grief?  And have I not—
Not one kind one on whom I can rely?
Lone, all alone.   No, not alone : his love
Shall comfort me although he may be gone.
But he is *not* gone—no, I know he is not ;
But were he gone, or were he proved untrue,
Yes, though he hates me I will love him yet."

Thus Nona bore an anguish in her heart
That none knew of : a bitter well of grief
That ever bubbled upward from those days
Fed from her thoughts, a constant running stream.

## MOREN.

NOW image is the food and bane of love;
For when it would nourish, it often, often turns
To poison, and so kills where it would cure.
And solitude is love's ally: the world
Holds it in check by turning the image away.
But thought on love alone unturned abroad
Is like that herb which puts the men who use it
Into such sleep whereof they neither die,
Neither do live, but lie in happiness
Sweet as the breath that blows across the vales
Into the world from out the dreamers' heaven,
While with the fumes the herb does turn its strength
To shake the soul with all the terrors of hell.

Before the warriors from their toils came back
Moren had left, and as he left forgot
Her and his love; for in the hurry and noise
His warring thoughts were turned from her and placed
Full on himself and on his hate; but when
The world in stillness closed about him he thought
Of Nona's face, and every fear was gone.
Then would he to his lonesome heart repeat
The words she often told him, how she loved.
But yet he had no power to face her now;
For in the using of the thought itself,

(51)

His life being drawn back to the baser world,
The fitful twilight of his mind ran fast
Into the darkness of his hateful self,
When ghostly voices mocked his vain attempt,
And called him coward and of meanly kind.

Changing he was, as changing as a day
In early spring, when promise first is given
Of weather fair upon the breaking hills;
When ere the sun is warm the clouds do come
To make a gloom where now we thought it fair.
And then we cannot prophesy with truth
For one short hour before us; and his thoughts
Were driven along around his brain as fast
As shadows chase each other over the fields.
He thought sometimes there were two powers within,
These ever wrangled, and one always ruled
With such an uproar as the gods had once
Warring with pride against the might of Heaven.
These were the race of Titans : these upheaved
The deep foundations of his little world.
Thus when he thought of her and on his hope,
The better ruled, and when upon himself
The evil one then tramped upon the good.
And since his thoughts were bent upon himself
The times were evil to him, and he lived
As lives a stranger in a distant land,
Who never hopes to see his home again.
Nor was it envy that possessed his soul,
Nor hate of any, but a hate so great,
So vast, so uncontrollable, so strong,
That single ones before him in this way

Were no more hated than a wriggling worm.
And when they had bound a captive of the war
Fast to a stake, and held their carnival
While offering up their heathen holocaust,
Then he, forgetting of their joys, dashed in,
Braving their menaces like a crazy one,
And turned the prisoner loose among them all.


When from a boy's hand high in air is cast
A stone, 'tis noticed how when at the height
It hangs an instant moveless without prop,
So stopt they as if shocked by some disease
At such unlook'd-for and peculiar act.
But only for a moment; forward sprang
The braves, and like a pack of hounds slipt loose
They closed around the wounded stricken game,
Which, after standing in bewilderment,
Had started off with instinct far remote,
As vermin when entangled in the toils
Try to be disengaged; but all in vain;
They were upon him ere he cleared the space,
And shouting dragged him helpless to the stake


To such it was a glory to evade
The watchfulness of captors, and escape
Back to their hills and glens, and issuing thence
Again upon the war-trail glut their fill
Of vengeance on the hateful foe to death.
But when escape was hopeless, then they sang
Their glory over, and reviled the ways
Of torture used upon them, calling it

A method fit for babes and not for men;
And if we give a credence to the truth,
We may believe a fortitude was shown
By these wild creatures, children all alike,
Even not surpassed by those divinities,
Those demigods and heroes that throng thick
The mythic page of them idolatrous.
Not she, the painted one, who spat her tongue
Into the face of her land's enemy;
Who had a statue in the open square,—
A tongueless lioness,—reared for her fame
Long since in Athens, could surpass their pride.

They brought the prisoner back, and made again
A circle round him of the gathered wood
From which the fire could barely touch the flesh,
Borne low and fork'd over the current air.
The sappy bands were bound around his waist,
And back behind the stake, crisped and black,
His hands were tethered fast; but from his eyes
A fire of hatred flashed and base contempt.
Then to the music of their own device,
With shrieks, and yells, and sound of rage delayed,
They tortured him to make him cry in pain.
But here the intent of that far-fabled lay
Wherein the wild swan sings its sweetest note
Yet heard in dying in its reedy home
Was realized by these.   Then their own homes,
Their squaws, their babes, their strivings after fame,
Their listless lolling in the summer sun,
The cheerful memory of the winter fire
Whereby the husbands laughed at idle fears

Told by the women from the far-off howl
Of hungry she-wolves seeking after prey
Along the borders of the desert land—
These they forgot, but knew if they should die
Like heroes, that their names would after live
In kind remembrance by their kin and tribe:
A thought collateral with the dying thought
That urged the saints to die a sacrifice,
They knowing that their life was not their own.

And such remembrance did not once recur
To him a helpless prisoner in their midst,
Nor did his memory run to once ago
When he stood up bravely; how hero-like
He clasped her as his own, and joyed that by it
There now had come a time to show his love.

They used this warrior badly as the rest.
They cut his ears out from his head; then each
That cut the members off, seized one of them
Between his teeth, and shook his head about
As dogs that worry mice; handfuls of hair
Were torn by jerking it from his helpless head,
And in his eyes was thrust a pointed knife,
Bent round and round, and twisted every way,
While strips of flesh were torn until they all
Had in their mouths a quivering bit of skin:
With these they daubed their cheeks, and frequently
They threw a bit out from the ring, to which
The children ran in scrabble; while the squaws
Would tell the youngsters how to torture him,
By casting coals of fire; this they would do,

Then, laughing at the sport, would run fast back.
And all this time they sang like crazy ones;
And he, too, all the time, sang tauntingly
The words next to his heart; and when they saw
They could not make him be a coward this way,
They jerked his tongue out of his mouth violently.
One thing they knew, and this they learned by time,
Which was to make the torture be severe,
Yet let the patient suffer under the pain
A lengthen'd life.   Yet he would not reveal
His suffering to them by a sign or way,
As to such death is sweet; but toward the last,
They did a favor as they loosed his hands,
Not meaning good; and when he felt himself
Loosed in the arms, he brought his hands aloft
And urged his fingers into the flabby gash
Above his breast, and tore a strip of flesh
With one last effort from about his heart.
He doing thus had purposed to reach in,
And with a dying effort seize his life,
And hold it to their view.   But death here stopp'd
      him.
Low down his body drooped; lower his arms
Swung near the warmer fire; and even here
They did not yet desist, but many ways
They brought disgrace upon the mangled corse,
By more unsightly ways than animals
That tear the carrion which the hunters leave,—
Far lower in grade than jackals that dislodge
The bodies buried in the lonesome wild,
Left by the travelers passing in that way.

And Moren they reclaimed likewise; and they
Would have dealt with him in their rage the same
As dealt they with a wolf when they caught one
Prowling about the village; but they were stopp'd
From using violent hands by other of them;
While some of his own kind, who knew his ways,
In order to appease the ones blood-hot,
Pointed with fingers and struck them on their heads
To intimate the place his weakness lay.
And gratitude, the tribute of the angels,
Did help to spare him in his time of need.
For once, and when a panther had seized a child,
A poor, slim, tiny one wrapped up in skins,
And made off for her den in rapid leaps,
Just as a cat would carry off a mouse,
Then he not thinking of danger to himself
Snatched up a club—the plaything of the babe—
Left in his speed the other ones behind,
Who sought for arms and implements of death,
And faced the wild beast as she laid it down.
He met the shock, bore her to the earth,
Drew the infant from the monster's fangs,
And in the mother's arms placed it.   She,
Wild and distract, worried the babe with kisses,
And almost smothered it up with tears, which brought
Tears to the eyes of those who stood around
Graciously; and they, knowing no other tie,
Remembered of it, looking for a time
In which they could repay.   Now was the time,
And for the present did they pacify
Their craving with it till they got him from sight.

But some were not to be put off by this,
And ere the day was over had they looked
To every corner peering for him : found,
They brought him like another captive, tied,
Before the chief, to whom they told the crime,
Desiring of him blood to wipe it off.
The chief then called a council, not before
It had been talked about and run the round
Of all the village ; by the talkative ones
Some things were added that did not belong,
As well as shortened when they told the truth,
But yet enough remained for all to know
That he should have to answer for his act
Before the chief and council of the wise.
Thus knowing they, through various causes led,
Came in a body to the council lodge
And filled the spacious room to its excess.

Upon a chair of curious workmanship,
Made out of boughs and antlers of the elk,
Set up above the ground upon a stage
That ran along the end of the room entire
Sat Oontum ; at his feet on either side
Were ranged the fathers whose consent was just ;
The offender and the offended to their right,
While to his left sat those who took his part.
Behind their backs against the rugged wall
Dead birds with drooping heads and outstretch'd wings
Were hung, all kinds from eagles down to bats,
And lizards also, and the skins of snakes,
And skeletons of the skulking, burrowing brood
Were stretched along the walls, and fleshless skulls

That showed their teeth and alway seemed to snarl
From many a perch, were in this curious hall.
These all brought reverence in the place they held
Clothed in an awe with power subordinate
To that Great One who ruled them everywhere.
A seriousness becoming well old age
Now rested on the faces of the wise:
With mouth set firmly with the edges down,
Scarce moving in their seats, they heard the case.
A warrior, one who felt the insult keen,
Demanded silence and the ears of all.
"Fathers," said he, "our cause is just. We braved
The many hardships of the fruitful war,
And brought a fame upon the common tribe.
Those whom we took were warriors well as we.
They fought like tiger-cats, and at the first,
Before the war turned for us, bore us back.
They helped to leave our braves dead on the field,
Whose bones the carrion crows pick, fighting for,
When we having our vengeance gratified
By taking pleasure at their snaky pain,
Thanking the Spirit for our great success,
This hunter here before us, one who hid
And rested free from danger and from toil
When we made haste to tear them from their nests,
Braved all the warriors in their dance of death
And cut the thongs of him bound to the stake,
While some that took his part then urged him oft.
What cause had he for this? What made him be
This way ungrateful to us for our pains?
Was it for this we tore them from their nests?
For this we carry the gaping wounds of war?

Was it for this we left our dead ones there
Whose ghosts still shriek upon the troubled stream
For those who injured and who struck them down ?
The wrathful talking of the evil one
Urged him to this, and now we ask his blood."

His party singularly groaned assent
Which ran around the room till it was stilled
By one who took upon him Moren's defense.
" Fathers," said he, " and braves, we hear the cause,
And pay due deference to your mighty deeds.
This witness by our help to torture those.
Mind how we tore the quivering strips of flesh
Clean down their backs, and helped to heap the fire
Within the hollow ; how we mashed their feet
Till the dark blood had burst the loosened nails
And hung the shreds upon the ankle bones ;
And when they told their deeds done in the fight
How we tore out their eyes, and cut their tongues.
Such is the feeling too of him before us
When he is at himself, but then the spirit
That has got angry at him in some way
Has turned a thunder-cloud into his head,
And made him do an act he could not help.
We cannot blame, for by his doing so
He made the pain last longer and more sweet.
This shows alone that Manito did do it.
We therefore ask you to be lenient,
And spare the hunter's life and let him go."

The braves impatiently then spoke through one,
" That the bad spirit did it is most manifest ;

That one it is which brings the evil days
Upon our tribe, and hurts us every way.
For this alone he should be sacrificed.
Who is it too that dare to ask his life?
Those ones who watch the women and the babes.
Let them go out and bring to us fresh scalps
Before they dare to talk, and when they fetch
A prisoner they can drink his blood themselves,
Nor we presume to tear him from their hands!"

The braves here shouted and grew petulant,
And high over their heads all through the room
Their flinty hatchets and their knives were swung.
Had it been elsewhere than within that lodge
The vengeance of the braves would've been upon him.
This even now was feared, for from the throng
A female with a child in upraised arms
Bore through the mass: she thrusted out the child
Towards their faces, and she told aloud
With rapidly flowing words that this was the babe
That Moren had saved to her and to the tribe—
To pity her, to pity him, and spare.
But still the voices were not hushed or quelled
Till high above the din came one loud scream;
Another female struggled through the crowd
Which opened for her as with one consent.

This one was Nona—Nona yet but changed.
She fell on Moren, drew his head to hers,
And for an instant lost herself to earth.
The crowd were taken back and sullenly,
As men whose rage is smothered but not quenched,

They stopp'd abased a moment wondering at it.
She raised her head; her arms were round his neck,
But with her hand she moved them back, and cried,
"Go back, you all; have you not blood enough—
So want to take more that is innocent?
And you, the chief, why don't you drive them off?
You have the power, and will you use it bad?
But yet you shall not—long as I have life
You shall not drag him off unless you drag
Me with him, and I care not then.   Stay back!"
His arms were tied behind him, so she clasped
Her own around him and she shielded him
With her own body in that angry time.

But Oontum from his massy chair arose
With anger so apparent that the cords
Of his huge neck were swollen twice their size.
He stood upright; his blanket loosen'd hung
From his left shoulder to his feet, looped there
At his right side was held fast by his hand.
His right hand clinched, his arm appeared all bare,
And so his nether limb, and on them hung
The uneven muscles in great matted piles.
He raised his foot and brought it down with force;
Into a blurry murmur sank the crowd
As he began to speak.   "What means this noise?
Why spoil the quiet council of the wise?
The cause shall they decide when it is told
By those wise prophets whom you all revere
Which spirit lies within him, good or bad.
So lay no hands upon him—let him be,
And spare the ingrate whom you all abhor."

So Oontum spoke, and they obeyed his voice
As from the room they all retired with speed.
Then turned he to his daughter : " How is this ?
I left my Nona ill, and she is here.
Up from that posture there and get you home,
Where women should be.   Let no child of mine
Ask me for mercy in a case like this."

The Eagle-Eye approached to Nona's side,
Clasped both her wrists, and loosed her tender arms
Like little withes of bark, and said unto her,
" Come, sister, come ; this is no place for you.
If still you want to get our father's will
You must not act like this, or he will think
There was no truth in any word you said."
When as he loosed her they bore Moren out,
She shrieking after them though she could not go.
They took her to their lodge where still she moaned,
With thoughts that they would kill him ; when she told
How he was all the love she ever had ;
From which they thought—poor, simple ones—that
      then
The evil spirit had likewise got in her.
Her brother here said to her, tauntingly,
" This is your love ; he is the one you said
Is worthy all of us !   A pretty one,
A common hunter and a coward at best!
What could you look for with the love you had ?
Shame, Nona, shame!   If I were bad
I would say, take him, and never see us more,
And this would be the worst thing I could wish."
Then when the truth was made apparent to him,

The anger of the chief was so inflamed
That words could not express it, but in his passion
He raved about the creature with contempt,
And in a breath forbade her have a love.

Then came alone those sorcerers who held
A reign of fear within their every mind.
The doors were closed with skins; a blazing fire
Glowed in the center of the chamber floor,
While round the fire a mystic circle ran.
Within the circle sat the conjurers,
Dressed in grotesque apparel ; one them had
Upon his shoulders swung a grizzly's skin
Of which the head was stretched above his own.
About the bottom of the skin were hung
A hundred tassels made of vermin tails.
Another had his head masked up all round
With holes cut in the mask for him to see out.
His body was smeared a black ; around his neck
In many a coil and knot were snakeskins stuffed
That dangled on his breast, and from his waist
He wore a garment as a woman's dress
Trailing upon the ground.   The third one had
Upon his shoulders set a wild-ox skull
Inversely, with the horns in front, and back
The jointed joy that hung down from its hinge ;
While to the skull in gathers was made fast
The ox's hide which hid its habitant
Without a shape within its blackish folds.

Long time they sate within the mystic ring;
No words were spoken, only now and then

One grunted like a beast; but at the last,
Rising involuntarily, they danced wildly
With droning howls heated in head and frame.
Then when they ceased, a fox was given to them.
They split it down and tore the entrails out,
Hurling them into the fire; then reaching coals,
Dropped them into the stomach of the cub
And drew the skin together, while they watched
The black distasteful smoke go up in wreaths,
And judged till now the omens were for good.

But when they came to separate the joints,
And scrape the white flesh from the loosen'd skull
To see the queer fantastic crooked lines
Which fire brings out upon the heated bone,
The signs were not so faithful or so good.
So on the coals were strewn sweet-scented leaves
Till the white vapor rolled along the roof,
While on the ground they moveless lay prostrate.
Again was all repeated, again they raked
The skull and bones from out the living coals,
And then they called it good : the oracle
Was pure and sacred, and no doubt was held ;
The wise believed and held it from above,
And told it to the people, who obeyed
Implicitly, and they pronounced him free.

When Moren from his prison-house was let,
Once more his ways came slowly back upon him
With thoughts of Nona and of better days.
She looking for him once again they met

6*

Within the suburbs of the scattered huts,
And then she told him of her grievances
With that devotion which the weaker have
To those the stronger whom they trust in love.
They promised here their meetings in the dark.
But seldom met they in their trysting-place,
Only by lonely times, for watch was set.
But one night—'twas the last one—there they met.
The watery moon went through the flying clouds
As if to catch the sunshine, while anon
Short, wild gleams shone flickeringly through the rifts.
There Nona rested lovingly her head
On Moren's breast, and Moren's arms were round
And held her nearer to his loving heart.

Then Moren spoke: "I know, my dearest bud,
That thou canst never be my own while here,
So I am troubled like the wind-drove waves
When storms set shoreward o'er our ferny lake.
Calm is the time of even, sweet the rest
Of night to tired, and worn, and weary ones;
But I am never happy, sweet, my dove,
While I am from thee, Nona, and thy love."
Then looking upward to his eyes she said,
"No, Moren, no, say never from my love:
The lonely dove does never cease to mourn
When from its side its mate is carried off."
"But, Nona, it can never, never be
That we are one so long as we stay here.
Then leave your father in his wrath behind
And seek a home with me far in the wild:
There will I raise a lodge where we will live,

There I'll be happy when I see but you,
There will we rest in peace, there ever love."
Then Nona, kind of stopping in her speech—
"Oh, Moren dear, you are my only hope,
And I'm unfit to claim your loving heart.
My father loves me, and he holds me dear
Almost to death; but then his hate, you know,
Is almost past one's suffering. Should we go
Deep in the forest distant from his sight,
My father's rage would surely find us out.
A man can go whichever way he wants,
But woman, she is weaker, and for her
To break herself against a parent's wish
Is but a lingering death. We are trafficked off
As things of no avail. But you will wait,
Just wait a little, Moren—I have hope;
Perhaps my father will relent for me;
If not—if not—" thus turned it off scarce knowing,
"Then we will leave and I shall do your wish."

Then Moren spoke as if he was surprised,
"And not till then? till then?" That was enough:
The doubt that fell upon him at that time
On such a mind was nothing but despair,
And thus the prospect of those other days
Was turned into a vision of the night.

But Moren still continued musingly,
"I see it plainly what the Spirit means:
We'll never know each other in the world.
But when my spirit passes to that land,
And thistle-down is blown from off my grave—

If I do have a grave—then will I come
And call you; and be with you till you come.
Then when you come I'll take your hand in mine,
And we will pass adown those smiling vales,
And live among the happy evermore."


In an instant after this the Eagle-Eye
Sprang through the bushes.   He ended their peace
By parting them and bidding Moren go,
Nor ever talk to Nona once again.
He said to Nona, " Were you not forbid
To see this hunter—by your father too?
This is the way his child does mind his voice.
Come on with me from this."   So carried her
With lengthy steps and left the other stand
Inactive at the suddenness of it all.


That night he wandered round, he knew not where,
With eyebrows raised, and with a wild, lost stare;
No consolation for him, as no grief,
That he could call a grief, was patent to him.
Little he cared to either live or die,
For in his franticness he knew no pain
This lasted through the day: no food he took,
Nor sleep the next night to his eyelids came;
But when the morning came, upon a knoll
That looked upon the village down, he stood
As flashed the flood of light across the land.
He heard the bluebird sing, and from the wood
The Indian-hen's long clatter reached his ear.
Then Moren, on the lodges looking back,

Where all was peace, and seeing the vapor curl
From out the lodges slowly toward the sky,
Let drop his head upon his breast in pain,
And turning his back upon them, wildly fled
Down through the desert to where the beasts abode.

When on some lonely isle far in the deep,
Through ways unseen, two human ones are placed
Who hold no commerce with aught living else;
When both together live for many years
Until they are bound by a stronger tie than blood;
When one does die and still the other lives
Alone and solitary—so Nona felt
Since Moren's self unto her had been lost.
And when the moon had waned and got her full,
And waned again and got her full again
A few succeeding times, a change did come
On Nona, which was noticed by them all.

She wandered round among them, but alone—
Alone like many where the crowd is great—
And felt in heart, if feeling could be told,
Like that one in the fable of the birds
Whose feathered mate was by a hunter killed,
But which still sate upon its native bush,
And from its little throat told all its grief:
And none could comfort it; and even the man
That struck its comrade would not strike at it
And in his mercy put it out of pain;
Till unsustained, it, dying in its grief,
Fell from its perch, and so went to its mate.
So dying slowly thus she was to them.

Her fretful sleep was short, and broken up
With dreams as changing as the many forms
That lie within the kaleid in the hands
Of a playful, careless child.   Then from her lips
Would come such words as, "I am with you now,
Moren," or, changing, " We are bartered off
To those who give the most, but I am thine ;"
While ever did his last words, like a plaint,
Seem nearest to her heart and tongue, and when
No one was near her studiously she spoke,
" And live among the happy evermore."
Her cheeks, so full, so healthy, now were sunk,
Their bones worked outward as in some disease ;
No more so springing was her active step,
But shorter, and her eyes were always down,
Nor after scarcely any more she smiled,
Save when some dear one, knowing, tried to please ;
She then dissembled, but never in her heart.
Then in these days the bud was withering.

And many hearts were sad and sorrowful
To see her wandering in the dusky gloom
At evening all alone, a shadow like
Of her that walked before ; or in the morning
Ere the Milky Way was dimm'd, while shone
The six lone sisters just above the belts,
Then walked a spirit on the bordering wood,
She whom they loved, now lost and comfortless.

Those times when word was but the law they had,
They all revered it as of binding force,

Sacred to death, and punished those with death
Who dared to offer such indignity
Right to their gods, in face of other men,
As trifle with a word when it was out.
So Oontum's promise given was held unasked,
While with the past these months were slipping away.
Then thinking that a change would change her ways,
The deathful knell was rung into her ear
Once more: once more was that dark day brought
     back,
And in a time before another war
That was expected on them after awhile,
She promised, to appease them, to agree,
With some faint hope she had, untold, infirm,
Perhaps only the shadow of a hope.
So those who thought within a little time
That they could not be swerved and all was sure,
Were forced by her sweet pleading to relent.
Such is the power of love on feeling minds,
Such is the power of women over men,
Such, over strength, the power of innocence.

But she was lost to every outward thing.
With her thoughts lifted from reality
She lived within a region that was dim,
Dim and uncertain, with no solid ground
On which to rest from weariness.   So time
In its old grooves of day and night slid on
Until the summer in November month
Brightened the faded garments of the wood,
And made a hazy covering for the hills
Which hid them from the frost, and brought again

The blue-jay from its covert screaming loud
Its lonely note from every leafy bower.
To her unheeded all, for not with sight
Or hearing do we love the outer world,
But with the senses of our godly part.

# IV.

## NONA.

THEN came the cheerless winter wrapp'd in mist,
  Bearing on Nona like the friendless mist
Old age sees from his eyes.  She went sometimes
A venture from the village for a way
To stand upon a hillock, with a hope
That that long-absent one, he hovering near,
Would see her, and then come and break her thrall.
But him she saw not, but she saw instead
The white land dinted by the cloven hoofs;
And still no friendly form broke on the sky
To meet her.  All in vain.  The low, dark clouds
Rested upon the haze: the river flowed
Noiseless to regions in a warmer clime
Under its ermine belt, and on its hills
The trees were green beneath their caps of snow.
And seldom in the day came sounds, except
A brood of wild fowl skirting on the wood
Struck up their clamor, or those wanderers
Across the zenith, coming from the north,
Trumped out their lonely call so desolate,
And drearer from a distant sky—still dimmer,
Till pass'd they from the sight toward that bright bourn
Where all is summer far beyond the seas.

7

Still came he not.   But once, when she had looked,
And seen him not, turning aside her head,
She saw on sudden on the horizon off,
A troop of bison like a fallen cloud,
For size and darkness, covering all the vale.
And fast it grew still larger, and she knew,
When all the plain was darkened, that she stood
Direct before them in their mad career.
She screamed, but useless: on the air it died,
Nor left an echo; as she tried to run
Her limbs refused her, and through nervousness
She sank upon the ground ; her power was gone,
And all her strength was in her strength of will.

But as the herd came bellowing over the plain
Pursued by hunters, at an angling wood
Saunup and three of her brothers, with some braves,
To tire their stiffened limbs broke for the brutes,
And veered them, but not knowing, from their course.
They joined the chase, and bounding fast along
Upon their rackets, scattered round the herd
Upon its sides and flanks to hem them in.
Saunup was there to the left, and passing close
He saw the darkened bulk lie on the snow.
To it he ran, and lying at his feet,
Her face upturned against the leaden sky,
Was Nona, whom he loved, seemingly dead.
He stooped to her and kissed her for the first—
Such kisses come not from the lust of flesh,
Nor ever are repeated ; and when man
Has pass'd his boyish days and come to man,
Then kisses for the first, earth is not earth.

From suffering long the throbbing of her heart
Was weakened in her, and the smallest fright
Made it beat fast, taking away her breath.
So she was helpless, and she lay as dead
When Saunup came upon her; but the chase
Swept like a wind along beyond the knoll,
And Saunup was with Nona left alone.
He tore the bear-skin from about his neck,
Threw it on her, and took her in his arms.
Then rested on his shoulder that sweet face,
Now cold and passionless; there hung those arms
Lifeless about his neck: then that big heart,
Which sent the crimson life-blood through his frame,
Beat fast and hard though soft now as a child's.

He bore her to the village: gently-like
He laid her down within her father's lodge.
There watched beside her till the returning heat
Sent the warm blood through all her veins again.
Then lifting up her eyes she saw above
The eyes of Saunup peering in her own,
And felt they looked of love, and in his touch
Was softness that belonged to tender hands.
And she rebelled not at his kindly way
Till to the sight of things her vision turned
And opened on the ravings of the brain.
And in this state she lay for a long time,
Tended by loving hands, till by their skill,
In helping nature to regain its sway,
And her own meekness, she came to herself.

So Saunup was another from the thought
" She loves me now from knowing how I love,"

And feeling thus, he fed his wayward thoughts
With food as sweet as honey to the taste,
While she lay lingering on her restless bed
Hid from his sight and distant from his voice.

But as the golden bees in summer time
Within a far wood in a deep ravine
Stored up the labor of their sunny hours
Inside a hollow tree, and then flew home
To brave the winter when it dared to come;
When with the first blast of the howling storm
That swept across the wood, down came the tree,
When all its precious treasure lay exposed,
And all their summer's labor lay as lost:
So Saunup's passion lying near his heart,
Though rich and pure, was as it had not been.

For Nona, though she hated no one, yet
One, only one, could claim the love she owed,
And other love was vain.    But yet she felt
A gratitude for Saunup for his love,
Which she could not repay or tell him of.
It hurt her much to see one claim her thus,
And so she pitied him—(and pity too
Is but a love)—and even wished a chance
Wherein her pity could be shown to him;
But then to do that what her father said
Was hateful, and she shuddered at the thought,
And with it life became a kind of pain.

But when the winter was almost with the past,
And from the south the peering sun came forth,
Telling his power upon the feeling earth;

When the old crows came circling in the air,
And followed soon the silver mocking-bird,
To sit behind the bush and laugh his fill,—
Then on a day most part the tribe went forth
To gather herbs and clay beside the stream,
While others chased the hoofs along the plain,
And some wove garments in the sunny town,
Against the war made by them on a foe
That lay far eastward o'er the morning hills.

Far upward from their stationary abode,
Within that valley by the river shore,
The monster stream swells out beyond its banks,
Making a lake among the craggy hills
Large and expansive.   Likewise in that age,
When doubt and darkness dwelt within the mind,
Gloom hung along the edges of the lake
Like on the fabled stream of Acheron.
The waves frisked listlessly against the base
Of mountains which the water had split like a knife,
Whose sides were covered with the firs and pines
That found a turf upon the jutting rocks.
But on the summit of a precipice
Highest of all, from which one looking north
Could see the waters of the lake expand
Beneath him, and its boundary gloomy green
In the far distance, and could see below
The wheeling eagles and the birds of night
Clutched, sleeping in the dark, to rough-edged rocks.
There was a boulder like a table spread
Over its top, and this was Maiden Rock,
But named thus after this.   Along the beach

Were strata of the earth from which they got .
At stated times the pigment that they used
For covering of their skins for war and art.
Hither with others on that spring day came
Nona, her father and his sons, and braves,
And made another home less permanent
Along the lonely coast.   Nor worked they fast,
Nor urged the business, but converted it
Half into pleasure.   While the squaws and boys—
A goodly number—helped to do the work,
Some others sat quiet where a patch of light
Bore through the leaves, and some along the shores
For pastime dangled high the scaly fishes;
Some practiced at their arts ; some lay them down
At full length by the fires, from which arose
Sweet sav'ry steam that quickened thus their taste,
Thoughtless and careless each to all save self.

During the two days now while they were there
Nona had roved along the sounding shore,
When looking once along the crags she saw,
Cut fair against the sky the rock's outlines,
Far up, and marked the gloom that lay beneath.
Then did the dark thought cross her soul, the thought
Of death, and with it ending of her pain,
For soon the day she promised would be here.

Nor all this time had Saunup been at rest,
For he loved Nona, and he told her so ;
Tried all his wiles to please her, softened down
His fiercer nature thus to catch her ear,
And did his best to make his feeling felt.

She used no harsh word to him, for she knew
It was her father's and her brothers' wish
For her to think of no asperity,
But, on the opposite, to hear his words
That she should please him thus ; but by no act
She hinted at, nor did she intimate
That she looked on him with that burning love.
Her face could not look bright while beat her heart
So mournful, but it wore a settled look
Of melancholy—sickness of the heart—
That sickness which eats inward at the core,
And makes the mind grow more and more diseased.

For when she would think upon the day now near,
Think, also, of the troth she plighted once ;
She shuddered at the doom that was reserved,
And mourned the more, and with it hope grew less.
But from that dark thought was her mind made up
In secret, and she kept it to herself,
Thinking upon her change while others slept.
This nerved her, and she felt another life
Grow on her sunken face, another light
Flash from her eye, and then a purer thought
Kept others in subjection, which was this,
That to the voice of Moren she would go.

So, leaving them, she wended her lonely way
From out the little campment, and she passed
Along the darksome dell and felt the waves
Plash up against her feet upon the stones,
And heard their endless music come and go
Monotonous.   She took the path that wound

Up to the hilly bluffs above, through bush
And over flinty pavement, toilsome steep.
After her resting often by the way
To gain her fluttering heart, and trembling sore,
Like a hurt bird that scares at every noise,
Thinking that they would follow, at last she reached
The weary summit.   Here she felt secure.

In going upward Nona had been seen,
And when she was missed by others in the camp
They asked with wonder where had Nona gone?
Her going up the bluffs was told to them.
Her brother felt uneasy at the news,
Imagining that something hung upon her,
And that some evil would befall her there,
So far from them in such a dangerous place;
And thus suspicion, undefined and dark,
Brooded upon him.   When they cast their eyes
Along the crags they saw her stand alone
Near to the edge—just hanging, almost over.

Then quick as thought he bid some follow him;
And springing far in many a rapid step,
Their bodies checkered here and there the green;
While Oontum with the others hasted fast
To reach the base, and all the camp appeared
Like to the outpouring of a swarm of bees
In April sunshine, while the murmur grew.
In looking upward as they ran along
They saw her gesturing with her arms far off.
Then all the women threw their arms aloft
And screamed to her, and moved her back with their
          hands,

And when her father at a distance came,
He shouted loud to her in his agony,
Scarce knowing what he said, or hearing scarce:
"Come back, my Nona, 'tis thy father calls;
Come back to this old heart that loves thee yet,
Nor Saunup's arms, but Moren's shall be thine."

She heard him not, but lifting up her voice,
She sang her death-song in that solitude:
"I go, I go,—for why should I stay here?
My love has gone away, and in that land
I'll meet my love again. See, there he stands,
Across the stream of death, holding his arms
To catch me. Fear not, love, they cannot take me,
For here they will not come. Farewell to all;
Father, farewell,—you killed my love with love;
Brothers, farewell,—no love like thine but mine;
And mine is stronger—for I overcome
Your love with love. Life without love is death;
Death with love is life: thus I get to life.
Oh, far across the plains I see the lodges
Where we shall rest; and thou, Great Spirit, come,
Come bear me 'cross the way, come hold me up,
Lest that I fall; and, Moren, hold your arms
To catch me to you, for I come, I come.
Now I am with you, love, for all, all time."

Ere the last words came from her lips she sprang
Far from the rock towards the stream, and fell
Down the long space, her arms extended wide.
At last she struck a crag; her body fell
Dangling along the bushes till it struck

Once more, then splashed into the waves below ;
Nor yet the echoes ceased to replicate,
But answered each along the watery caves.

Too late had those ones come—too late to save.
They at the top had seen her body fall,
Had heard her dying song of grief and love,
But could not save.  They neared the brink, but shrunk
From it far back and held their eyes from day.
Those at the base who sought to take her up
Saw her fall from them to her lasting grave.
They hasted along the shore : there Oontum came ;
Twice had she risen to the water's edge ;
The third time, when her features broke the waves,
He saw her, ghost-like, with a bloody gash
Cut in her forehead, and her hair spread out,
Floating like snakes around it.   When it went
The third time down he never saw her more,
Nor any one saw her more, although they looked
With wishful eyes for her, and dragged the stream
With toilsome hands, but never more they saw her.

From this time forth Oontum was changed in mind :
That last dark sight had made a wreck of it ;
Nor could he ever through the coming days
Think on the world as he had thought before.
For time had made quick feelings to grow slow,
And like the rust eats in upon the iron,
Remorse corroded fast upon his heart.
And not long after was this old man seen—
For in a short time he grew old and stooped—
With head bent to the earth, plodding his way

Through the long avenues and the aisles of wood
That led from round the town to quietness.
But everywhere he went he saw her face,
Her laughing voice he heard from many a nook
Sing in the windy music of the leaves.
Then when he thought the vision always changed
Into that last one when he saw her face,
Then would he start, and stare, and beat his breast,
And rave out on the hard heart that he had,
Which would not for her sake one time relent.
This could not last, and so he died of grief
Who laughed at grief as but a woman's lot.

So ended all his wars, and when he died
The tribe, as was their custom, honored him
In costly burial with their sacred rites.
Three nights they howled around the blazing pile
On which the warrior rested in his death ;
The warriors living danced around the fires,
Droning a requiem, while the women sat
Deep in the shadows, wailing forth their hymns
So dismal, sad, and full of ghostly words.
Then on the coming day when the new sun
Shined through the wood in all his fiery red,
Two youthful and manly hunters out were led
Across the green to where the chieftain lay.
This was a sacrifice they always made
To their dead chiefs—they were to follow him
Down those dark regions through which, after death,
The ghosts descend to reach the hunting-grounds.
Then after the perilous passage was quite over,
And crossed the angry flood which separates

The fields of light from pain, they all would rest
In other homes upon the happy shore.
They looked so innocent, and a light serene,
Such as the martyrs wore in olden times,
Came from their faces, conscious of their doom.
Then being led with fettered hands around,
They bowed their heads as to an altar down:
Then swung two war-clubs in the morning air,
Down they were swept upon the kneeling ones:
Then came a twitching and a spasmy gasp,
When on the ground, for twice or only thrice,
Then a long quiver, and they both were dead.
Neither was marked, but little rills of blood
Dropped, trickling, from their nostrils to the ground.

They lifted up the dead, and wrapped them all
In blankets and in skins, and laid beside
Each one of them the weapons he had used,
That they might have them in that other world.
Thus they were buried in a kindly hope,
And over them all were heaped the earth and stone.

But never more they heard her trilling laugh
Sounding so merrily in their company;
And never more she past the lodges gray;
And never more they blest her as their own;
And over the tribe there came a sudden blight
As a dark shadow on a wedding-day
Makes those ones shudder who are most concerned.

The children missed her too, and often they,
The little hearts, would ask with tenderness,

To know where Nona was these many days,
When catching grief would make the big hearts swell
With softer answers, "Nona has gone to rest."
And like the drone that lingers in one's ears
With never-dying echoes, little griefs
Make sorrow seem the greater, as the shell
That lay for many days upon the coast,
Lapped by the ceaseless waves, does tell,
In a faint mimic, to the villager
The endless sounding of the barren sea.
But yet her brother's grief was worse than all:
" Sister," he would say often, and the word
Sank deep into his heart, seeming to mock,
" Sister!"—" O mine, whom I shall see no more,
Whose life I killed with love, or rather hate,
Say will you not come to me e'en once more,
And shake your black locks o'er my sleeping face,
And wake me with a kiss as you did once,
In happier days, and laugh my grief away?
Never, oh never, and I am the cause."
And in the stifling of his inner grief
His grief grew at the telling, and his thoughts
Involuntarily would wander back
To their sweet childhood days when both of them
Were playmates on the green to when they stood
Beside their mother on the wigwam floor
To listen to her songs of other days.

And Saunup had no word to say about her,
But he likewise did often walk alone
To kill a thought within, and get from where
The places spoke of her in silent tongues.

But yet upon the others of her kin
Sorrow spread out her wings like some huge bird,
And much they felt to know they were the cause
That brought the trouble by unkindliness.

So the trail of war they joined one time more,
But with forebodings which they never had had.
This time they were successful but in part:
The youngest brother they had left unfound,
And Saunup, their ally, they brought with them
Upon a litter, dead—all sorrowful.
Thus little joy was felt when they returned
To see them coming home without the one,
And with the other lying on his bier.
He on the bier they placed within the square;
Whereat, like Oontum, he lay out in state.
Up to his waist was drawn a robe of fur;
His lithe, long body, all bedaubed with paint,
No covering had; upon his hilly chest
One arm was placed, the other dead one drooped
Down his lank side.  His war-decked head hung back,
Leaving his large, red mouth hang open, while
His wound of death, a gash above the eye,
Gap'd staring, and in it one could run a hand.

Another time they danced around the dead,
Sung their low wails, and fasted day and night;
But in the day they built a funeral pyre,
And on it laid the body in its dress,
With all its fighting arms and scalps about it.
Then in the middle of that gloomy night,
As on the corse many a fitful gleam shone,

The chieftain seizing a brand ran to the pyre,
Which caught the shining flame and wrapp'd the dead
In many a livid fold; and with the smoke
That started from the greedy fuel's touch,
An eagle loosed, flapp'd free its cloudy wings,
And sought the sky, its native home and haunts.

The days from this time grew monotonous,
And many wondered where had Moren gone.
For when he parted he left no trace behind,
But past into the wild, there made his home,
Surrounded by the wild beasts till he died.
Alone he died—no friendly hand was near;
But no one doubted this that Nona's ghost
Hover'd about him as he lay, and sang
Sweet music to his ear to ease his pain,
A prelude to that music of the skies.
And eaten was his flesh, and in his bed
His bones lay whitening, and he was forgot,
Till one day by some hunters straggled out
The bones were found lying within the cave,
Unhurt, alone; which, when together put,
Made up the skeleton of a long-lost man.
There in the fragments hanging round the neck
A little wristlet made of polished bone,
Tied to a thong, was found: this Nona 'd worn,
But later was a relic of her love,
And by this clew they knew whose bones they were.

Then near the cave was scraped a hollow urn
In which the relic and the bones were laid,
And over these was raised a mossy cairn.

Soon, very soon, the seed fell 'mongst the stones,
Then was the barrow hid by grass and weeds:
But many a song the owl did love to sing
In gloomy night-time when the moon shone dim,
As if to keep the dead one company,
While timid foxes burrowed underneath,
And reared their young ones by the hollow skull.

But after many moons a voice was heard
In night-time in the soughing mournful wind,
When winter held the earth within his web;
And to them in their straining it appeared
Soft, plaintive, low, and seeming far away,
Like chiming bells far out upon the sea.
This they do say was Moren's restless ghost
Come back among the lodges once again
For Nona from the distant Spirit-land—
Yet some did hold that Nona was there with him.
These times the little young ones huddled close
In round their mother while she told the love
Of Nona and of Moren and their doom.

Long after this it was before was formed
That mystic worship which they all confessed
When all of them retained their household shrines.
Then slow by slow did this one learn its own.
Then generations with their ceaseless tramp
Followed each other, still they held for truth
That Nona's body lay there in the lake,
And that those lights which skim along the swamps,
Which one can never catch, was Oontum's spirit;
While the fire-bugs that glimmer in the mist

Just after twilight were the rest of them
Who helped to hunt her body in the waves.
Moren was turned into the whip-poor-will,
That gloomy bird which hides his head from day
And sings alone at night his song of woe,
Hid in some vale beyond the homes of men;
And what was more complete, they always held
That higher, where the stream foams over rocks,
Making an endless spray—where ceaseless mist
Rises above the cataract's groan, and clings
To the smooth surface all along the shore
For distance, was the Good Spirit's earthly home.
And so the water was sacred, and it seemed
The grave had been ordained for her who slept
Within it, and the place itself so grand
Was but an altar built without frail hands;
And to a late day, when they come from wilds—
Descendants of the ones who lived around—
With no pure worship in them, standing there
They are subdued and passive, nor they leave
Without an offering of the incense herbs,
Or little relics which they hold most dear,
To satisfy the cravings of their god.

And furthermore, to all the tribes far round
It grew a spot well known and long revered;
And such a passion lay upon the place
As lies upon the homestead, seldom seen,
But never once forgot by most of us,
With all its quaint surroundings, where our feet
In childhood tramped in innocence and love.
And they full credulous believed each tongue

That spoke the prodigies shaped in the brain,
Not unharmonious with their simple ways.
Then every bird that trimm'd its glossy wing
Among the swinging branches of the pine
Sang of the love of her, and any swan
That ruffled up the eddies on the stream
Would not be touched, such was their reverence.
And when the fall wind swayed the heavy boughs,
And bent the rushes bordering on the lake
In rolling waves, they fancied that they wept
In unison for her; and every leaf
Talked in a language of their own like birds,
Of that fell story of their wayward love.

A remnant of this tribe long after left
Their hunting-grounds along the river shore,
And past together in a huddled band
Still westward toward the mountain's sloping base
Which like a parapet circles round the land
And holds it from the sea—that boundless sea
In whose far waters every night for years
The sun was buried to their darken'd eyes,
Or went to ghostly land; and where they lived
Was made the haunt of many a forest beast
That got its food by night and lived by stealth,
Till in good time a people blest of God
Came across the ocean, settled in the land,
And made the wood to be a feast for eyes.

But to the scattered ones it is a spot
As sacred to them as is a mother's grave
To orphan children in the light of truth.

The Indian maiden, thinking on Nona's love,
Does to her memory often drop a tear;
While many a brave far in his forest home,
Thinking on her sad fate thoughtlessly turns,
To think of other times, fortunate days
When nature was untrammeled and they were free.

When evening comes, and night drops on the earth,
Or through the stars the moon looks sadly down
Upon the water to its shadowy rim;
When in the north the winds are laid to rest,
A sound comes from the rock-cleft overhead—
Softly and sweetly from the distance comes,
Echoing from rock to rock, from ledge to ledge.
The warrior stops, now dressed in peaceful dress,
Yet firm believes that it is Nona's voice.
The hunter on the water on the lake
Sees then a dim form leaping from the ledge—
Or if he does not see it, thinks he does—
And falling, falling far down in the dim light
Until the darksome shadows swallow it up,
Or in the misty moonbeams it is lost.

And he believes it when he thinks upon it,
For when an infant he was lulled to sleep
With that same old tradition by a voice
That rests now covered by the moaning wind,
But which still sings beyond the narrow grave:
And he believes the echoes of that voice
Before the voice of any living one.

And then within her bush the whip-poor-will
Stops her song: the listener stands moveless,
Trying to catch the echoes dying off
Upon the quiet waters in the hills,
Like to the strings of some old instrument
Moved by the careless wind—till all is gone.